This
Bear with Sticky Paws
book belongs to:

CORA RITCHEX

KEEP YOUR PAWS OFF!

D1399264

tiger tales

an imprint of ME Media, LLC

202 Old Ridgefield Road, Wilton, CT 06897

This paperback edition published 2010

First published in hardcover in the United States 2009

Originally published in Great Britain 2008

by Orchard Books

a division of Hachette Children's Books

an Hachette Livre UK Company

Text and illustrations © 2008 Clara Vulliamy

CIP data is available

Hardcover ISBN-13: 978-1-58925-081-9

Hardcover ISBN-10: 1-58925-081-8

Paperback ISBN-13: 978-1-58925-424-4

Paperback ISBN-10: 1-58925-424-4

Printed in China

C&C0110

The Bear with Sticky Paws

Goes to School

by Clara Vulliamy

tiger tales

There's a girl named Lily
and she's walking very slowly.
She says,

"I don't
want to go to
school today!"

"Hurry up, Lily," says Mom.
"We'll be late!"

"But it's just too boring at school.

I've got no one to play with.

I want to stay home!"

And—

CRASH!

—down goes
her bag!

But then, ding-dong!

At the door is a bear—a small, white, fluffy one—standing on his suitcase to reach the bell.

"Come to my school!"
says the bear.

BEAR
SCHOOL

BEAR 1

"It's FUN at Bear School!"

"Do we hang our coats up here?"
asks Lily.

"NO!" says the bear.
"We throw them in the air!"

"OK," says Lily.

"Sit down, everyone!" says the bear.
"Are we all here? Lily?"

"Yes!" says Lily.

"ME? Oh YES!" says the bear.
"Now, let's get started...."

"What will we do first?" asks Lily.

"PAINTING!"

says the bear.

Lily paints

1 red house, 2 orange cats,
and 3 yellow ducks.

The bear paints

1 BIG BLUE BEAR.
And—oh NO!
Sticky paws everywhere!

"MUSIC TIME!" says the bear.
"Oh, good!" says Lily.
The bear plays ALL the instruments—

1 pink piano,

2 tooting trumpets,

3 crashing cymbals . . .

and 1 great big drum.

And—

oh NO!

Too noisy!

"Time for COOKING!"
says the bear.

Lily makes

1 gingerbread man,

2 chewy brownies,

and 3 cupcakes.

The bear makes
1 BIG GOOEY MESS.

 And—oh NO!
Sticky paws everywhere!

"Is it story time?" asks Lily.
"YES!" says the bear.

"Blah dee blah
la
dee
dah..."

"That's not the story,"
says Lily.
"No more story!"
says the bear.
"It's dessert time!"

"It's nice to share," says Lily.

"Not share!"
says the bear.
"ALL FOR ME!"

"I want to do my numbers," says Lily.

"I want to do CARS!"
says the bear.

And—oh NO!
Everything gets knocked over!

"Let's play grocery store!" says Lily.
"What would you like to buy?"

"EVERYTHING!"
says the bear.

And—oh NO!

He runs off
with the cart.

"Wait for me!"
says Lily.

"OUTSIDE!"
says the bear.

And—oh NO!

CRASH!

Down comes everything!

"That's *enough*," says Lily.
"I'm done with Bear School.

I want to go to
my school.

GOOD-BYE!"

"I'm ready," says Lily.
"Wait for me, Mom."

"Let's go!" says Mom,
holding her hand.

And Lily hops,

skips,

and jumps

all the way to school,

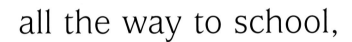

arriving just in time...

to wave a happy good-bye...

and make one new friend.